"…and the Big Bad Wolf huffed and puffed all the way home."

It's the same old story. Wolves are crusty, lazy, and mean.
They howl, they chase, and they make a mess.
We know all about big bad wolves and their nasty ways…

Don't we?

Crumbs

Grub

Hairball

Scribble

Knits

Yoyo

British Library Cataloguing in Publication Data
A catalogue record of this book is available from
the British Library.

ISBN-10: 0340 88411 8 (HB)
ISBN-13: 9780340884119 (HB)
ISBN-13: 9780340884065 (PB)
Copyright © David Melling 2006
The right of David Melling to be identified as the author
and illustrator of this Work has been asserted by him in
accordance with the Copyright, Designs and Patents Act 1988.
First edition published 2006
10 9 8 7 6 5 4 3 2 1
Published by Hodder Children's Books a division of
Hachette Children's Books, 338 Euston Road, London NW1 3BH
Printed in China

For Marianne, Alex, Rosie and Daniel.

Love to Monika and Luka.

Thank you to Igor who patiently drove me
to the four corners of Dugo Selo.

Plus a special thank you to Geraldine Stroud.

THE SCALLYWAGS

Jumble

Earwax

Brooz

David Melling

h
Hodder
Children's
Books

A division of Hachette Children's Books

It was a full moon and the Scallywags were late, **again**.
The other animals had arrived early and were dressed in their best.
But now the photographer was tapping his watch.

'We can wait no longer,' he snipped,
'or the beautiful silver light will be
gone and the picture will be ruined!'

He peered into the lens one last time.
'Say **cheese** everyone.'

'Cheeeeese!'

'CRASH!' 'BANG!' 'WALLOP!'

The wolves bundled into the camera, the photographer and the other animals.

'You hairy **nincompoops!**' yelped the photographer.

'Typical wolves,' mumbled the others.

The next morning, the animals gathered around to see the photograph. They were so cross that they decided not to ask the wolves to eat breakfast with them.

'They'll just **spoil** it for everyone,' said the moose.

'I agree,' said a bear. 'They always flick the food and nibble the napkins!'

'I sat next to one of them at supper time last week,' said a pig.
'He was SO smelly, I couldn't finish my pudding!'

Meanwhile, the wolves were loafing around at home.

Jumble, the leader of the Scallywags, gave his tummy a prod.

'I'm hungry,' he said. 'What time is breakfast?'

'Dunno,' said Earwax, 'but I can smell it!'

The pack wagged their scratchy tails, pointed their **twitchy** noses and trotted after the delicious smells.

But when they arrived, the other animals had already finished.

Everyone had enjoyed breakfast without the wolves so much they decided to stop asking them to all mealtimes.

And playtimes.

And storytimes.

Soon the Scallywags were not invited out at all. At first they didn't mind, and they carried on doing all the things that wolves like doing...

But Animal Larder wasn't the same without...

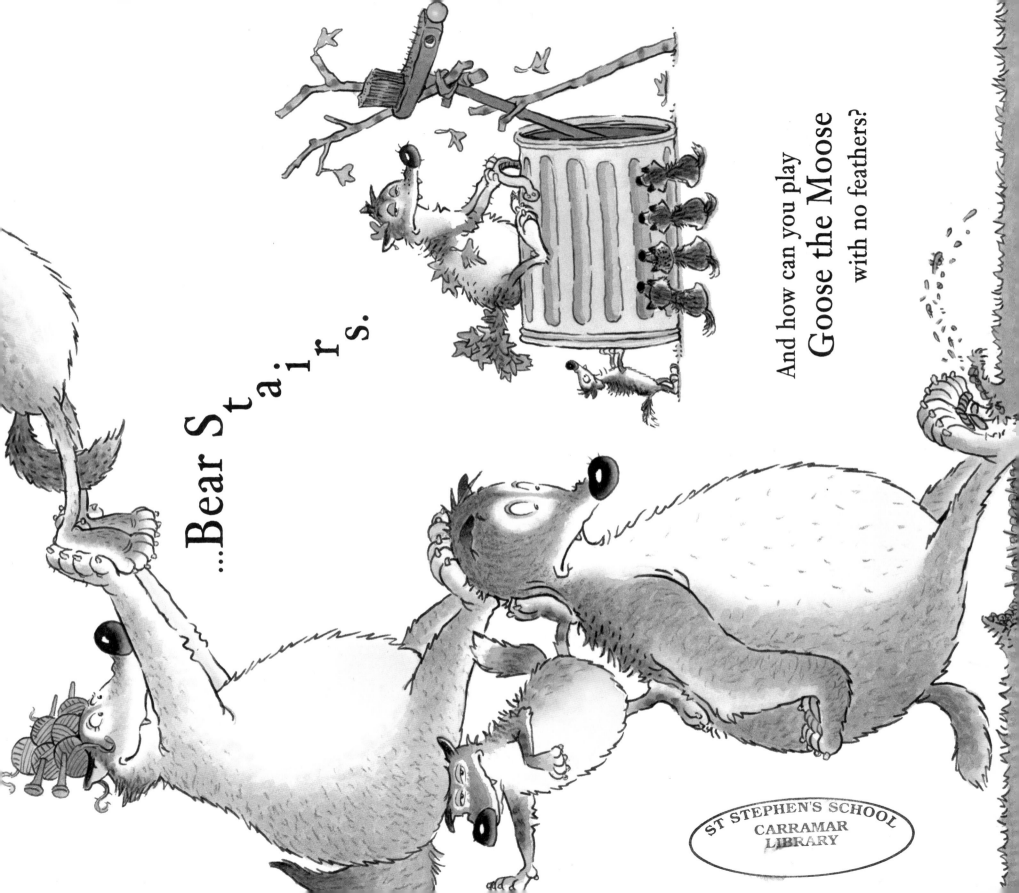

...Bear St a i r s.

And how can you play **Goose the Moose** with no feathers?

'What we have to do is show everyone that we aren't so bad,' said Jumble.

'Yeah,' said Brooz, 'no one gets to see our soft and cuddly side.'

'Maybe if we had better manners!' coughed Hairball.

'But we don't got no manners,' said Scribble.

YoYo sniffed his armpit. 'I suppose we could have a bath.'

'And I could make some nice clothes,' said Knits.

Jumble sat up – 'I know, let's go into town, follow the other animals around and copy what they do. Then they're bound to like us!'

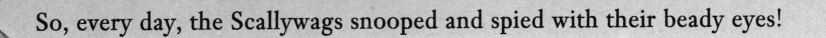

So, every day, the Scallywags snooped and spied with their beady eyes!

And every night they practised very hard.

Before long **most** of the wolves knew what to do with...

a handkerchief,

a toothbrush,   and a comb.

And **some** of them could dress nicely and say *please* and thank you.

And so came the day when the Scallywags decided to visit the other animals and show them how much fun wolves can be!

The animals were delighted to see fourteen tidy visitors dressed in clothes that spangled.

They didn't recognise the Scallywags and asked them to stay for a bite to eat.

But no sooner had the soup arrived than the **trouble** began.

Scribble leaned across to one of the pigs and smiled sweetly.

'Excuse me,' he said, 'please don't slurp your soup, it gives me wind.
Thank you so much!'

It didn't stop there. The wolves checked that all the animals had washed their hands, paws, trotters and claws.

They told the geese not to **honk** with their beaks full and a family of bears were reminded not to leave the table until everybody had finished.

The animals soon changed their minds about the fussy guests and began to realise how much they missed the Scallywags.

'Of course the wolves are noisy,' they whispered, 'but at least they're funny, and they can enjoy themselves without telling **everybody else** what to do!'

Above them the moon came out. A full moon.

The wolves became restless – they loosened their buttons.
They started to itch and they started to scratch.

Grub pressed
his elbows into
a sandwich...
on purpose.

Scribble giggled.

Crumbs nipped
YoYo's toe.

Earwax squashed
a pea on Jumble's nose.

Hairball's tail pop^{p}ed out
and Knits bit it. He yelped.

Brooz howled. They all howwled.

'The Scallywags!' gasped the animals.

For a minute nobody moved. Then Jumble coughed –
'Would anyone like a sandwich?'

'Yes please!' they said and they all tucked in!

The animals were so busy enjoying themselves that they forgot to
be cross with the wolves. And the wolves forgot... well, everything!

The photographer smiled and set up his camera. 'Ready everyone?'

'Cheeeeese!'